Oh,
It's You, Buster Grimes!

William E. Oliver Jr.

PAGE PUBLISHING, INC.
Conneaut Lake, PA

First originally published by Page Publishing 2021

This is a work of fiction. Any resemblance to anyone living or dead is merely a coincidence and the results of the author's vivid imagination.

ISBN 978-1-6624-3215-6 (pbk)
ISBN 978-1-6624-3216-3 (digital)

Printed in the United States of America

I was born in Providence, Rhode Island on the East Side. The East Side had once been the White section of town, but the only Whites who remained there were too poor to move away and so lived among us. I lived in a big house at Eleven Admiral Street, on a hill directly across from the black elementary school, Bennet Street School. I had a mom (Leslie E. Grimes), a dad (Walter E. Grimes), and two sisters. One sister was nine years older, and one sister was two years older. The one who was two years older was Janice N. Grimes, and the one who was nine years older was Bernice F. Grimes. I also had one brother, Arnold S Grimes, who was fourteen years older. My brother got confused at times and thought that he was a second father instead of an older brother. My father worked for the federal government at a Naval Yard, and it was in full swing since World War II was just ending when I was born. Most of the White men of that era had a stay-at-home wife, so because of his "good government job," my father thought my light-skinned but still-Black mother ought to stay at home also. We owned a barn and a vacant house as large as the one we lived in. The vacant house was falling apart with the help of boys who played in the "haunted house."

I began to notice girls at an early age and had a preference for long hair and light skin. My father had told me that I needed a good looking light-skinned Black woman with big legs and a big bust to be a success. He told me that I had to learn the games of the wealthy. I was to learn golf, tennis, swimming, chess, and also a card game named bridge. He told me that the other Black boys could chase wealth by basketball or some other sport, but in reality very few make it that way.

At age four, my dad had told me that he had a child that was still alive named Walter E. Grimes Jr., and I was named Walter E. Grimes Jr. But I was healthy and the other sickly. The sickly one would never do anything that my dad was proud of in his life.

My father would get my sisters, my mother, and me up in the middle of the night and talked about maybe putting us all out of his house. My brother was off to the Air Force. My sisters cried, and my mother looked worried, but I played with my fingers and toes. My sister thought I was able to play because I did not understand, but what they didn't know was that I understood all too well. I was my father's pride and joy, and my mother needed to be there to take care of me; however, she would not agree to take care of me and lose the rest of her children. Therefore, as much as he huffed and puffed, nobody was going anywhere.

When I was five, my godmother brought a little five-year-old around to the house. She was light-skinned with a pretty face and big legs. I was told to "give Ronnie a kiss." Her name was Veronica. I grabbed her and dipped her and kissed her hard, and everyone was surprised, but my father only smiled.

I went to the Black elementary school across the street and tried to be good, but there was one bully who was a girl. If you beat her, first you had to listen to the crap about not hitting girls, and then her brother (who was fourteen) came and beat you up. It seemed like I was her favorite target.

In the second grade, I stayed back in kindergarten because the teacher said I wasn't ready. I had drawn a purple horse and would not change it, and the teacher said, "You cannot put a square into a circle." My agile mind got a small square and placed it in a large circle, and everybody laughed. I was told I was not ready to go to the first grade.

Because my father had more money because of his "good government job," we had the first television in the neighborhood. All the nearby children declared that they were "my friends" and came to my house to watch the *Howdy Doody* show. This included the girl who liked to beat me up. So in the first and part of the second grade (as the other families got TVs of their own), I was left alone and even protected by the bully girl. However, once the others (including the bully) got TVs, I was once again the object of fights.

In the second grade, my mother had a friend with two children, and she and a prominent businessman (a member of the mob) were close. He forced the school system to accept her two children and their two cousins and my sister, who was two years older, and me. We went to the White-only school fifty-seven blocks away. We had to walk past the Black elementary school on the way to the public bus. The bus took us to the bottom of the hill that Sway Breeze School sat on. While at the White school, we were aware of how much we were behind even in the same grade and had to work hard to catch up.

They offered music lessons, and I took a clarinet (my father played the clarinet and saxophone in his band years). I was allowed to bring my school-owned clarinet and my music book home. I then had to play whatever song we had learned for my father.

At school, my music teacher turned to the page and played it several times. Whenever I messed up, she would point to the music and play it again. I watched her fingers and played each piece to her satisfaction. One day my father had a friend over and was bragging about how well I played. The friend asked for a song that I had never played and I asked to play one more familiar. The friend said yes. My father insisted. I had to admit that I could not play it because I played by ear and could not read music. My father was embarrassed and apologized to his friend and sent me to my room. My father had just bought me my own clarinet and saxophone but now was so ashamed that he sold both the next day. I continued in music class for the rest of that semester but never brought my instrument home again. Once the semester was over, I never signed up for music anymore. I was now caught up in school academics and was as smart as any White kid in my studies. My father was still proud of that. Back home when I wanted to play, I was told to "go play with your White friends." They had TVs of their own now and no longer needed to be my friend. I made my dad spend money on sports equipment like a real football and a real helmet. He bought a real bat, baseball, and catcher's mitt. The kids would be playing football on the playground across the street with an old tennis ball. When I asked to play, they said, "Go play with your White friends." I then went home across the street, got my helmet and real football, and stood on the sidelines until someone realized that I had a real football and a helmet. Then they said they didn't mean what they said and that of course I could play. Different people wore the helmet, and we played football with a real football. It was the same thing for baseball, same old tennis ball, and same remarks until I had a real baseball and a real bat instead of a broom handle. And I was their friend, and "Of course I could play." I learned at an early age the difference between an associate and a friend, and it served me well for the rest of my life. I became comfortable with my own company and did not need to "hang with the crowd."

My mother, Leslie, was one of six children born to a couple in Florida. There was a tragedy that deprived all six of both mother and father. It served as a traumatic episode in all of their lives and led to an alcohol problem for all six. This incident was hidden from me, and lies were told to me until I was fully grown. Leslie had Arnold and Bernice from another marriage, but my father lied. He backed up the date of his and Leslie's marriage to include Arnold and Bernice. Leslie never went to college but finished sixth grade (grade school only went to eighth grade back then). She lived through the Depression and talked briefly about how horrible it was. Black people had always been able to eat well on the underbelly of America, but then 94 percent of America was attempting to eat on the underbelly. Food, not much more than garbage, was scarce back then; so when Leslie found my father, through all of his faults, was a good provider for her children, she put up with his mess for the sake of her children. She had to sneak out and do daily work, which meant cleaning someone else's house, washing clothes and ironing, and other assorted things. Although he wanted a stay-at-home wife, he gave her no money.

Walter E. Grimes, apparently, was married before although he never directly said so, which accounted for his sickly Walter E. Grimes Jr. My father told me "stories" of how he was a great lover and had rich and poor women after him. He was not allowed to own a Cadillac but had a Buick Roadmaster (Cadillac company had declared that a Cadillac car was too fine of a car for a Black man to own and would not sell him one.) That being said, every White man had to have one because Black men couldn't have one. Because of this statement by a car company and the segregation of Whites in the Midwest and the South, Black men were being hanged for "reckless eyeballing" (looking at a White woman). It seems as though Black men from the South and Midwest set up two things as a measure of freedom in the North—one, they wanted to own a Cadillac car, and two, they wanted a White woman lover whom they could treat in any way they wanted—to show that they were truly a success and free.

When I was seven, my father told me that his sickly Walter E. Grimes Jr. had died, and I was now the only one. At the White elementary school, things had changed. There was a big White boy who was a fifth-grader, and I was still short and skinny in the third grade. This boy was the school bully and, by our understanding of fair, was also a "dirty" fighter. It was after he had beat up an acquaintance of mine and stomped him with his feet that I became angry enough to fight him. He was a head taller and twenty pounds heavier than me, but I was angry. He threw me down and tried to stomp me, but I grabbed his foot and twisted, and he fell. No sooner than he fell, I was all over him, hitting him in the mouth, eyes, face, head, and everywhere he was not covering up. The crowd pulled me off of him. We stood up, and I prepared to fight on.

However, he ran away, never to bother anyone the rest of his time there. I became king of the school that day and until I left. There was a new boy who came to the school, and he called me the N-word on the playground. Everyone froze. My second- and third-in-command said, "You hear what he called him? Get him." Twenty boys took off after him. He ran off, and when he approached school the next day, someone said, "There he is. Get him." Another twenty boys took off after him. On the third day, he came accompanied by a female adult crossing guard. She and he stood across the street where he pointed out which one he had insulted. The female said, "Young man in the green shirt, can you come over here where we can have a word please?" All the boys were at the fence watching and waiting for a sign. I went across the street, and she stated that her son needed to make an apology and an oath to never say anything like that again. This was 1953, years before integration. He apologized, and she asked me if that meant he could come back to school. And I said, "Yes, ma'am." We shook hands, and I motioned to the still-waiting crowd to disperse. She watched as they followed my hand gesture. No one else challenged the king of the school again (until junior high school). There were Black elementary schools and White elementary schools, but both White and Black had to go to the same junior high (grades seven, eight, and nine). There were not enough junior high schools to divide us up by color.

By the time I was nine, my sister Bernice, nine years older, graduated high school and wanted to go to college. My father told her that girls did not need college and to go get a job, which she did. My father drank ginger ale in two-liter bottles, and they were worth five cents at the store if cleaned. Therefore, for my birthday at age eight, I requested and got a long-handled brush. What does an eight-year-old need with a long-handled brush? Well, we had both mice and roaches (six bedrooms, one-hundred-year-old house), and the brush was to clean out the roaches so the store would accept them. I would clean twelve, and my sister wanted me to clean some for her. I lent her my brush and saved her some of the not-so-bad ones for her to clean as she had already shown me her true colors. By the time I was twelve, my other sister, nine years older, was getting married. And my father went deeply in debt to put siding on this mammoth house.

This house had a front staircase that went to the second floor, went to the third floor where there were four bedrooms, and up to the widows peak. A widows peak is the top of the house with glass windows on all sides, a place to stand and look at the harbor where the schooners came in. If her husband's schooner was there, all was well. If it was not, she was most likely a widow.

On the first floor of this house was a front foyer with a steel door and an iron grating in the door. There were two glass panels in the door that you could open without opening the door. If you went from the front door to the dining room, which was opposite a large den, pass that into a large eat-in kitchen. The house dated back to the 1800s and was said to be a governor's mansion at one time. The original house must have been the four bedrooms and four rooms below that and the widows peak. The living room and den had working marble fireplaces. The rooms above that had working marble fireplaces. The addition to the house must have been around 1900 because it had the apparatus for gaslights and a kitchen half bath on the first floor, half bath in the basement, and a full bath on the second floor. There was a back staircase to access the two bedrooms above.

Most of the houses in the area were almost as large, but they had been cut up to be fully contained apartments on each floor. They each had a separate bell, utilities, and everything. When people came to my house, they expected a cut-up apartment house but once inside became confused and envious and backed away from me. The neighborhood children who had watched my TV knew that they lived in a cut-up house and we lived in the whole house, which furthered the division among us.

My father did not make my life any easier, telling me to go to the back door and tell the kids to get out of the back house (haunted house). The kids would run when I yelled, but again these were the same children I was trying to play with when I had time. My father had more money because of his "good government job" but was not good at paying bills. He sat at his desk in the den all evening. I would hear him arguing with creditors on the phone. Phones at that time were party lines and usually started with a word like Dexter One. Later we got a private line (fancy, fancy). All dial phones were owned by the phone company.

As I grew older, now eleven, I was still short but suddenly began to get fat; so I was now short and fat. It was then that I was told Ronnie (Veronica) was coming over for a visit. I was upstairs putting on all three belts to try and hold my stomach in and still breathe. I came downstairs, and there was this pretty, long-haired fat girl. I was so glad that she was also fat that I went and took off the other two belts and could breathe again. I still dipped her and kissed her, and she smiled.

Black men from the Midwest and South had set up, as a measure of success and freedom, two things—one, they wanted to own a Cadillac car, and two, they wanted a White woman as a lover whom they could treat in any way they wanted—to know that they were a success and truly free. Therefore, to my father from the Midwest, it was no great surprise that he took on a White woman lover with three small boys. Later when he voiced his desire for a Cadillac, he was talked into buying a Lincoln Mark IV instead.

My father was forty-two when I was born and so never played any sports with me, but we did play chess twice a week (and he won each game). He would tell me how important it was to win with grace and lose with grace. We played chess from the time I was nine (twice a week) until I was thirteen. Two times fifty-two equals 104. One hundred and four times four years is equal to 416 games. Finally, when I was thirteen, I won one game. He said I needed to find someone else to play. Four hundred and sixteen times he won, and one game I won. And that was fair?

Arnold S. Grimes was my brother. He thought of himself as an artist and was pretty good at it. When he wrote letters from the Air Force, being eighteen years old to twenty-two years old and me being four years old to eight years old, he put cartoons in it to make it fun. He was out of my life early with him being so much older. He came back long enough to go to the Rhode Island School of Design (RISD), and we played horse with the basketball (horse is when you stand in one spot and shoot) when he took thirty-minute breaks from studying.

Bernice F. Grimes was "the sarge" because she was nine years older. She was often in charge of us when our mother snuck out to do day work. In our house, you could go from the den into the living room, to the front hall to the dining room, and back to the den (a complete circle). And once I knew that if I pressed Bernice's nose in that she had to pull it back out, the game was on. I would innocently go by her and press her nose and start running. And I was fast. Even though I was nine years younger and had no knowledge about a women's parts, I knew enough not to bother her when she stated, "If you want to live, then you better not bother me for the next three days." One time I pressed her nose and ran with her close behind me, saying, "I'm going to kill you, so help me."

I stopped abruptly and turned and asked her, "Why should I help you kill me?"

We fell on the floor and laughed madly.

Another time as I approached, she saw me coming, held up her hand, and said, "You are too young and unsophisticated to understand the mentality of my philosophy. Now go away, little boy." I spent the next two days at the dictionary figuring out what she meant.

My other sister Janice was two years older. When she stated that she was in charge, it was a declaration of war. "You're not in charge of me," I would say, and we would fight. My sister was short and fat; I was short and skinny. When we fought, if she was able to sit on me, then she won because I could not move and had to give up. If my small fists were able to pound all over her and then she quit, when Dad got home, I would get a beating for hitting a girl. I figured it out—fight and win then lose to a beating when Dad came home then fight and lose and lose twice to a beating when Dad came home. Therefore, I stopped fighting her and just ignored her. I didn't do what she said and sometimes got a beating for something she was to make sure that I did. When we were younger and both my brother and sister were home, we (the little ones) were always blamed, and Janice would ask if I did it. I would answer no and ask her if she did it. She would answer no, and the result was that we both got a beating. Five times I asked her if she did it. And I didn't do it either, but the two older ones said we did it. And instead of both of us getting a beating, I told her that although I didn't do it, it made no sense for both of us to get a beating and took the blame and the beating, and she got none. When I asked if she would take the blame for a change, she stated, "No, I'm not getting a beating for you, and you most likely did do it even though you said you did not." No sense of fairness there.

At the junior high school (the White school and the Black school had to send their sixth-graders to the seventh grade). The White school, me included, had a 7.7-grade equivalent in knowledge. When the Black elementary school sent their sixth-graders to the seventh grade, they had a 4.6-grade equivalent. For some coming from the Black elementary school, they never caught up. Thus, our class played and joked as we were taught information that we already knew. The others tried hard to learn, but they had not been taught. Some teachers understood their plight and tried to do make up to help them catch up. Most teachers just expected you to know.

By the time I got to junior high, I began to grow rapidly. And all the fat evened out. In gym class, this boy heard I was king of my school and hit me. I did not respond except to block his blows with my hand. He thought this was funny in each gym class. As someone distracted the gym teacher, he slapped me around. Until that morning that my mother made me not just angry but also flat-out mad, it was gym class day; and when he tried to slap me around that day, I yelled, "Not today, fool!" and proceeded to hit him and knock him over from the front of the locker room to the back. I had blacked both of his eyes, and he was fighting for his life. But I was fighting harder. By the time I stopped and he ran away, the crowd whispered, "That's why he was king of his school." I had met two new young Black men, and I knew one from the White school. I stated that we call ourselves the Fabulous Four (years before the Beatles) and all the girls said, "Okay." And we turned to one another and said, "It worked." We stated that we would always be friends. Two of them from the East Side and one from the West Side (rough side of the railroad tracks). My friends were John Plumber, George Clinton Bentley, and Robert East.

While at the White elementary school, lunch was an hour because the White kids went home to their stay-at-home moms nearby, but George and I were far away from home. We walked to the store where we (Black kids) were allowed to be in and had mostly peanut butter and jelly sandwiches (no refrigeration for our sandwiches). However, at the junior high school, there was a cafeteria where all of us ate. We tended to sit at or near the same tables all the time. Near one of the tables we sat at, there was a short, frail White boy; and he had mustard and potato chip sandwiches to eat. I had a meat sandwich, a peanut butter and jelly sandwich, a piece of fruit, and a dessert for lunch every day. One day I went to his table and took Jonathan's (little White boy) sandwich and told him I would trade him. He said, "Okay." I took his mustard and potato chip sandwich and threw it in the trash. I then gave him half of my meat sandwich and half of my PB and J sandwich every day. As members of the Fabulous Four went to sit with the girls, I ate alone. Sometimes a girl would come over, and sometimes Jonathan would come over.

I had grown rapidly and now had some height and some weight distributed nicely along with my form. The story of the fight in gym class had spread, and no one bothered me until ninth grade. By now I was quite popular with the girls, and the question loomed large: Who would I take to the ninth-grade social? But before I got there, it was one more fight. It was winter, and snowballs were fun but not slush balls. Slush balls are mostly frozen water with snow on them. A guy hit me with a slush ball, and I was after him. He was more than a head taller and thirty pounds heavier. But my reputation has spread, and he ran. I told him an apology would end it. He stated that "he did not apologize to anyone," and that meant we had to fight. We squared off in the street, and we danced around, and I fought him and blacked both of his eyes and swelled up his face (I looked untouched). He came to school the next day with sunglasses and was told to take them off until the teacher saw his black eyes. He was then allowed to wear the glasses that day.

CHURCH WORK AND GIRLS

I was an altar boy from the time I was five years old until I was six-teen years old. Many families with both boys and girls attended the church and knew me well. We were to have a church picnic at an amusement park; however, that Saturday, it rained and rained. We all went into the church basement. Someone put on a record player, and some of the girls danced with each other. For the guys, we started eating the picnic food. I saw two girls dancing whom I knew well and "cut in" (to cut in is to tap the guy on the shoulder and ask, "May I cut in?" and sometimes with no words, just the tap on the shoulder). Just then a girl with a full figure (hips, breasts, and all) tapped the girl on the shoulder and cut in to dance with me! Well, I figured that was because no other guys were dancing. We danced, and I sat down. I cut in again on the two girls I knew well, and Ms. Full Figure cut her out again. Fully shaken, I sat down in the corner after that. She (Ms. Full Figure) came over and sat with me, so we talked. We said, "Too bad that it got rained out. It would have been cool." We said that there was a big movie in town that everyone wanted to see. She said that she wanted to see it too and that I should pick her up at 2:00 p.m. the next day, Sunday. I stated that I didn't even know her name, so she told me. I stated that I don't even know where she lived, so she told me. Her name was Valerie Stealer, and she lived on Tenth Street.

I went home after that muttering softly, "I have a date? I have a date?" I was thirteen and my sister Bernice was working and visiting my mom. She heard me, so she gave me some money. She told my mother so she gave me some money. My mother told my father, so he gave me some money.

The next day, I put on my suit and tie, put on some comfortable shoes, and walked over to her house. I met her mother, who told me she heard so much about me (strange, I had only met her daughter yesterday). We left for the movie and could have taken the bus, but she said it was such a nice day, and we had the time and should walk to the movies. We started walking, and she grabbed my hand and started holding it. I pulled away and put both hands in my pocket, then she took my arm. Hands out-took my hand; hands in-took my arm. I finally walked along with her holding my arm. Suddenly as we passed the Anchor High School field, I saw (it seemed) all the guys I had ever known on the other side of the street. They began to yell, "Hey, Romeo, how's your girl?" Then two or three said, "That's not Romeo. That's Don Juan!" And they proceeded to call me Don Juan for another two blocks. My nickname was Buster, but for years my alternate name was Don Juan, usually shortened to just Don. Over the next couple of years, anyone hearing me answer to Don looked confused. I'd tell them, "Long story. Don't ask."

While we walked to the movie, the same thing happened—my hand, my arm, and I just let it be. We got to the movie, and we got a large bag of popcorn and got caught up in the movie. Whenever I turned in excitement to say something to her, her lips were almost on me, and I quickly shoved the bag of popcorn into the vacuum. I got through the movie without kissing her, and we went outside.

The outside was wonderful! It was dark. You ask me, "What's the big deal?" Dark meant that we couldn't walk home and instead took the bus. (I didn't have to hear all the guys again.) We took a bus back to her house, and I came inside. Her mother asked about the movie and then said, "Well, I'll leave you two young people alone, and she went upstairs." (She too had a full house, not a cutup). I wanted to cry out, "Wait, wait. Don't leave me alone with your daughter."

I sat on the edge of the couch. She squeezed in next to me all breast and shapely hips. I moved over away from her, she moved over toward me, me over, her over, until I got to the other end of the couch, trapped. In desperation, I grabbed a framed picture of a skinny little girl and asked who she was. Valerie stated that it was her two years ago. I looked at the image of the skinny girl and all the hips, breasts, and narrow waist of this pretty girl next to me. I tried to figure out how this could be. Finally, I asked her how old she was. She was *eleven*! She had a better figure than my sister who was fifteen at the time. Her mother, thankfully, made a noise upstairs, and I turned and looked at the ceiling just before her lips found mine. She also looked up. By the time she looked back down, I was at the door, saying, "I'd see her again sometime." That was my first date.

WORK

I had put in an application for a paperboy at age twelve and not gotten it. Therefore, I shoveled snow and did odd jobs to earn "legal" money. It was December 6, 1958, when I got a call that a boy had quit and left a prime paper route open. I was told I should come at five forty-five the next morning. My mom got me up, and I dressed as warmly as I could, not knowing what to expect. The owner of the paper office had a list of my clients and how they liked their papers. I didn't even know how to fold paper. So the owner and another adult told me to get into the back seat of a large car with all these newspapers and his list. We drove to an area (walking distance), and he was teaching me to fold papers and throw them close to the door and which ones to go and place in the screen door. Well, a strange thing began to happen. I found envelopes marked to the paperboy with money in them. Wow! Before January 1, I had $235 in envelope money from my route, and I was sold! I used some of the money to buy myself suitable clothes and shoes to be out in the cold (Providence, Rhode Island, in winter).

I bought an alarm clock but slept right through it, which my mother in her wisdom realized, so she would be awake when my clock went off; and if I did not respond to the clock, she would yell at me and give me a whack or two with the belt. Well, it got to a point where whenever that clock went off and I didn't move, I was whacked with the belt. Finally, I would wake up as soon as the clock went off. I would wake up and tell her, "I'm awake" to avoid that whack with the belt. After a couple more weeks of this, I would wake up as soon as the clock went off, and I would say, "I'm up," and no one would be there. I had learned to wake by the clock (with much help from my mom). I went to my paper-route clients and asked if I could do odd jobs at each house. Some (most), said no, but some (a few) said yes. One house with a large-framed Irish maid employed me most. I was liked by the man and the woman of the house, and they often invited me into their living room while they imparted some bit of wisdom that I would need in life. I trimmed their hedges and cut their grass every week in spring and summer. There was a little White kid about six or seven years old from next door. He tried to talk to me as I worked, but I didn't have time to stop and listen. Therefore, I solved the problem. I lifted him to my left shoulder, and he sat there and talked to me while I worked. I put him back down when I had to go uphill and put him on my shoulder when I was level or going down. He was there every week when I came except this one time; he wasn't there when I came. His sister (about my age) came over as I was cutting grass and stated that her brother was sick that day. He looked forward to the next time riding on my shoulder and talking to me. And she asked me to come next door and say hello. He was in bed because of some illness and looked sad but became all smiles when I went to his bedroom.

I continued my paper route even after my mother tried to get me to quit to go on a family trip when I was fifteen. However, my father stated that "I was learning the New England work ethic," so I stayed with my godmother while they were gone. I could not get someone to deliver my route for those few days and give it back. Most wanted the route for themselves. I was cutting grass, trimming hedges, and cleaning out attics; and I started at the paper office Saturday night inserting the sections into each other. Sunday paper had most of the same inserts each week, but we had to wait for the new section and then insert the inner part into the news section. We worked all night into Sunday mornings. I began missing church as I was too tired to work all night get two hours of sleep and then go to church and serve on the altar. Every other week, I did do both but slept most of Sunday after that. I had figured out that not all of my paper route clients celebrated Christmas, so I had cards made up to say, "Season's Greetings," from your news carrier and put one in each door at Christmastime. And the tips improved.

By the time I was fifteen, my sister Janice was graduating high school and wanted to go to college. My father told her that girls did not need to go to college and just go and get a job. Janice had never worked and had no money. Neither Bernice nor Arnold could help her, and Mother had no money. However, I had money sitting in the bank that I had earned. My mother explained that my sister really wanted to become a teacher and needed to go to college to do that. She asked could my sister use my money to go to college. I told my mom that I intended to live out my dreams, and I wanted my sister to live out her dreams as well. My mother thanked me, but my sister never did say anything even close to a thank-you. I continued working like that, and by the time I was seventeen I had saved again enough money to buy a car. My father had to sign for it, but I made it clear that it was to be my car.

LEARN TO DRIVE AND BORROW A CAR

When I was thirteen, I thought that I knew everything! I asked my father for some money (my money had been put into the bank), and he started on his lecture about how "money doesn't grow on trees." I said, "Yes, it does. There is a money tree in the front hall." (We had a dried flower called a Japanese money tree with round silver leaves like silver dollars in the hall.) First, he rolled up his fist to hit me, and I closed my eyes and stood there. Then he opened his fist and was most likely going to slap me. Then he took a deep breath and stated, "Then you go and spend some of that money," and walked away.

When you are about thirteen or fourteen and full of yourself, you think everyone else is a dummy. Jerry Lewis, the actor, had a movie called *The Jerk* where he did stupid things. Therefore, when we were thirteen or fourteen and were busy doing nothing, we called it jerking off. My brother, fourteen years older, called and asked me what I was doing. I told him, "Just jerking off."

He was stunned and said, "What?"

I thought to myself, "Gee, Buster, your brother is so stupid." So I explained, "Jerking off, hanging around, acting like a jerk."

He laughed and said, "Oh."

It would be two more years before I learned another meaning, and then two years later, I felt stupid.

Well, when you know everything, of course you can do anything, right? (Maybe not.) I had been given car keys (my own set), and my sister Janice had been given car keys her own set to use when we went on some boring trip to the "Shriner's" convention. I thought that since I had car keys, that I could drive. I had watched my father put the car in drive and then drive away. Since I got out of school first in junior high I was alone to drive the car a few blocks and then put it back without anyone knowing. However, when I put the car in drive, it would not start! So that meant that I knew almost everything but not how to start a car. I watched my father put the car in park or neutral and start the car, shift to drive, and then drive away. *Now* I knew everything (I thought). The next day, I got home even earlier as I ran most of the way. I got the car keys and started the car. The car was at the front end in the driveway, which meant I had to back out. Now I sat here to think if it turned like my red wagon or not. As I sat there, the elementary school let out. I put my foot on the gas, put the car in reverse, and *stomped* on the gas. The car shot out and hit the big tree in the rear bumper and cut off. The school kids laughed at me taunted me, saying, "You can't drive, ha ha." I was going to put that car in drive and go the forty-five feet to the bottom of the hill. The crossing guard was helping children cross the street at the bottom of the hill where I would have to stop, turn left or right, and proceed without killing anyone or myself. My guardian angel (her name is Gwen) told me that if I turned the car down the street, I would kill about five children and the crossing guard. Then went across the street and into the house at the bottom of the street and kill me as well. She showed me a picture of what that would look like. I was now scared and sweating in the middle of winter. I just wanted to put the car back despite the children taunting me still. Now the problem would be to miss the big tree, miss the stone column on the other side, and miss the house. I turned the wheel to aim back into the driveway and stomped the gas (no idea how much pressure it took to move the car). The car shot forward, missed the tree, missed the stone pillar, and hit the house with the right headlight. Holding the brake pedal with both feet, I let up enough to back up two or three feet and straighten up a little. The car was too close to the wall to get out on the driver's side. The front door on the passenger side was jammed, so I had to climb over the seat and go out the driver's-side back door. I thought to myself, "Maybe nobody will notice." I was frightened to death and thought of running away. But I remembered last year when I attempted to run away and saw my father almost cry. I knew I could not do that again, so I had to face the music. The music sounded like a death march right then. My sister Janice got home. She noticed and said, "Dad is gonna kill you. Can I have your comic book collection when you're dead?"

My mother got home next and found me in bed under the covers. You see, there is something magical about bed covers. They can't kill you as long as you are under the covers. However, when they peel the covers back, then you are dead. My mother, in her wisdom, told me to confront my father and tell him my feelings after I told her what happened. I told my father the whole story, and he suggested that I should name my own punishment. I felt so bad that when I turn sixteen, I was not going to ask to drive (I was almost fourteen). I told him I should be grounded until I am forty-seven years old. He smiled at that despite how angry he was, and that was that. He went out the next day and got another newer car.

NINTH-GRADE SOCIAL DANCE

By the time the ninth grade came on the radar, the fabulous four were all the talk and as the leader of the fabulous four everyone wanted to know who I was going to take to the social. Some of the girls secretly had bet on who it would be. I wasn't supposed to know about that so I pretended not to know. East Providence was across the red bridge. For the most part, that group dated someone from that group only. But the four of us were known near and far. I used that fact and invited Judy Awkward to my ninth-grade social and blew up all bets (the bets were all girls who went to the same school as I did). We took pictures, and the teachers and the principal were at the dance. The principal was a little crazy and had a twelve-inch ruler that he stuck between couples so we were not dancing too close. We really knew the principal was nuts when he wanted us to waltz to the song "Alley Oop."

SUMMERTIME

It was the summer between junior high school ninth grade and high school tenth grade. In America, the racial picture had not cleared up. So instead of going to camps, we went to visit our relatives in a different city. Last summer, it had been Harlem, New York, where my cousins lived in buildings that connected and had a common roof. This gave the internal security guards a fit when we dropped balloons filled with water on their heads. When they chased us, running into one building, we ran three buildings over (on the connecting roof) and came down the stairs in another building as if innocent. The summer before that, I had been in the Bronx, where I had to join a gang called the Eight Aces, although there were about forty of us that particular summer. To join the Eight Aces, we had to jump off of a billboard into the ground covered by broken glass. But the only clear space was the size of a trash can. We either climbed the ladder and jumped or climbed the ladder and were pushed. Oh, by the way, I was sent to my family in New York because number one, that is where most of my family lived; and number two, the recreation center was around the corner where a boy was heard to say, "DAMN!" And my parents did not want me to expose *that* (little did they know [I smile]). This summer, the one before school, I got to stay home; and when I was not playing with my junior high school friends and acquaintances, I was working my paper route and doing odd jobs. This particular group that had formed during junior high school was playing baseball (real bat and stuff), and we were playing on Anchor High School lot. Someone pointed out that Sandra Blacksky had arrived on a bike. They were going to meet her and try and date her. I stated that I had not met her yet and would go also. That was when three of these young men tackled me on a baseball diamond, stating that "I could not meet her, or they would not stand a chance." So I lay there under the pile of three, and all of her would-be suitors put their hearts back in their chests.

Summer came and went, and now we were enrolled as "ten B babies, go wash your heads in gravy" entry level to high school at that time. I was in the library, minding my own business, when I got a note and the one who passed it said it was from a pretty girl. The note said, "Who are you? I have never seen you before."

I answered, "I am Buster Grimes. Who are you?"

She got close enough to whisper, and she said that she was Sandra Blacksky. She stated that I was kind of cute but too bad because she was going with Tony, a friend of mine.

I replied that Tony was not my friend, just somebody I knew. And besides, "I'm here now so just quit him and go out with me."

She replied, "Just like that?"

I replied, "Yeah, just like that."

So she did and went out with me. It was like that with most of the girls I met. Most wanted to know me before I realized they were really alive.

MY FIRST CAR

I was seventeen, still riding my black bike, and the boys were taunting me, saying, "You still riding your bike? I've got my driver's license."

I laughed and said, "Yeah, but I am riding on my bike. And you, with your driver's license, are still walking."

It made them mad when I said that. I convinced my parents that after paying out of pocket to go to a driving school, I should buy a car. My father took me to a place, and I bought a stick shift car (cheaper than automatic), although my father still had to sign for it. As luck would have it, I was cool—cool enough not to tell anyone that I had my own car. I would ride to their house on my bike and, once the date was set, pick them up in my car. I had two dates, one each weekend before my car (thirteen-year-old car) broke down in eight days. Word spread fast that I had a car, but since I had not shot my mouth off, when it died I was able to say it was my sister's car and not lose face. (Losing face when you are a teenager is a *big deal*.) So much so that two summers ago, back when repeated efforts by my father, Boy Scout camp counselors, and others, I still could not swim—that is, until several of us were in New York and playing tag around a large swimming pool with sixteen feet of water at one end. I avoided getting tagged, but there I was in sixteen feet of water. I could yell and cry and lose face or start swimming. I stroked across the pool like I had been doing it for years, got out, and kept playing (see no loss of cool points/losing face.) I was without a car for six months with my sign at the dealer that read, "He sold me a lemon." Six months later I paid some more money, but I got a newer stick-shift car, six years old. This time I still did not shout it from the rooftops but didn't deny it if asked if it was my car.

SCHOOL GRADES, PROMS, AND DATING

My name is Walter E. Grimes Jr., but most knew me as Buster Grimes, and some knew me as Don Juan or just Don. I ran track because I was fast (maybe from all those years running from my sister [I smile]). I got a school letter in Track. I played football and I got a letter. I was a two-letter man. There was the usual letter sweater that buttoned down the front, had blue on the straight collar, and all the way down to the bottom of the buttons. However, my letter sweater was pure white with a shawl collar and my letter on the side. No one else had one like it (I ordered from my brother's girly book). When you are a letterman in high school, you rate. When you are only one of the two young men with their own car, your own money, and a two-letter man, everybody knows who you are. I also had parties to die for—big six-bedroom house, invite only. I was "playing the field" as it was known then. I guess later it changed to just player. I was not known for going with any girls meaning going steady (only one girl). I was not into what the other jocks were into. They called it the Four F Club. Number one, find them; number two, feel them; number three, f——k them; and number four, forget them. I knew that if you got a young girl pregnant, you had to marry her, and your life was over. Many young men thought that if a girl gave it up (had sex) on the first date then. In their eyes she was a s——t and that she would give it up to any boy. My view was that for every 10,000 boys that a girl meets, she may say no to 9,999, but there is 1 in 10,000 for which she has no defense. If that one asked her to lie down with him, she will. I hold women in high esteem sexually but still played the usual teenage games. Since I was not (going with) any one girl, I had women/girls in different parts of town. For the most part, East

Providence was across the red bridge. And girls dated boys from East Providence only. However, I was mobile with my own car, and that meant I got to date girls in parts of town that others did not have access to. I said that there were two young Black men with their own car. The other guy was not a threat because no one knew who he was. They knew that he played in the band, was quiet, and had a blue car. I decided to find out more about the other car owner, so I had someone point out his car. Then one day I went and sat on the hood of his car. As he came up to his car (I had been given a description of the guy), I begin to introduce myself. He stopped my saying, "Everyone knows who you are." He told me his name was Saul Weakley, and he lived across town but had special permission to attend Anchor High. He invited me to his house to meet his mom. He told me that his dad had died in the past two years. I accepted his invite, got in my car, and followed him to his house. His mother was younger than mine. My mother was somewhere about fifty, and his was about thirty-five. And she was nice.

That era was the era of "sidekicks." The Lone Ranger had Tonto, his faithful companion, and every star had a sidekick. Saul became my sidekick, and soon everyone knew who he was. He was like two different people. When Saul was around me, he was funny, witty, and charming. When alone he was shy and quiet. When we went on double dates, he was funny as long as I was within six feet of him. When the girls went to the bathroom, they went in pairs or bunch. But when the guys went to the bathroom, we went by ourselves. Saul would be telling a joke when I got up to go to the bathroom, and when I got back the girls would ask me where the *string* was. They then told me that when I got about six feet away, Saul shut up and remained quiet until I was within six feet, and then he would start up again. Since I ran track, Saul tried out for track, but he didn't run fast enough or far enough. However, he was perfect for high hurdles and earned a letter. Much later, when he had his letter sweater and I had mine, we cut class at Anchor High (colors blue and white) and went to East Providence High (colors red and white). We walked around the school at lunchtime in our sweaters. Saul and I continued to double-date, but I could not double-date for my prom with him (more on that later). And so Saul did not go to his prom. I was a big-time jock, and although I did not engage in sex, still he did not do his own homework like the rest of the jocks. I usually chose well, someone with straight As, but chose poorly for senior English, only a B student but pretty. I was told by my teachers that I used to be a graduating senior but now would have to stay an extra semester to take senior English again to graduate. With my staying back and no longer eligible for sports, I was no longer top jock but still very popular. I graduated in January 1964 instead of June 1963 with the rest of my class. However, I went to the senior prom of the class of 1963. At the time I was dating a pretty girl, and her father had just begun to let me take her on dates by driving my own car. Before that, if I took my own car, I had to take her seven-year-old brother with us. This girlfriend was from another part of town, and her father had moved her to a different school. I was still playing the field I had a girl at Anchor High and her at her school. Saul and I had lined up the two young ladies for the 1963 senior prom, and we were going to double-date.

Meanwhile, I had met Edward Kennedy Ellington II, and we became friends. He graduated from his fancy private school with a prom on the same night in 1963. My sister Janice considered me and my friends to be children since she was two years older. She was, however, starstruck. And when she learned that Edward was the "nephew" (Duke said nephew; actually, he was the grandson) of Duke Ellington and when Edward asked her to his prom, she agreed to go.

Now Saul and I were going to double-date because when I asked the pretty girl's father and explained that it would be just me and her until the wee hours of the morning I fully expected him to say no. However, he fooled me and said yes even after I explained that we would be gone until 2:00 or 3:00 a.m. He still said yes. He said that she could go but had to double date with her male cousin. Boom, a grenade into my plans! That meant I could not double-date with Saul even though the two girls had already bought their gowns. *Now* what? New plan. I asked the White couple with the Irish maid if I could borrow the car for the prom. They had two cars, a new 1963 Cadillac and a large 1962 Ford four-door. My emotions wanted to say the Cadillac, but my intellect said the Ford. I would even be allowed to come over and wash and wax it the day before. I told my father that I would use their car, and the iron curtain came down. Boom! No, no, I was not to use their car; and I crossed my fingers on both hands and said okay (when you cross your fingers and tell a lie, it is not really a lie). Well, now Janice and Edward were going to their prom and a pretty girl with her male cousin. We were going to our prom, and that made six people. My father offered to drive one set (my sister and Edward), and I was to use my car for the four of us. However, we said no and that we would manage. That night, Edward walked to my house to pick up Janice, and I left to pick up the other three. What really happened was I parked my car on a lot of Anchor High, walked over, and picked up the 1960 Ford. Then I picked up the pretty girl and her male cousin and his date. We went back to the lot and parked beside my car. We got out and got into my car. We came home for pictures after taking pictures at the other two girls' houses. My father again offered to drive Edward and Janice, and they said, "No thanks, we like it this way." The three girls were in their gowns and in the back seat, and the three guys were in tuxedos and in the front seat when we left my parents' house. We drove to the parking lot and agreed on a time to meet back up. Then Janice and Edward drove away with Janice driving my car. The rest of us were in the 1960 Ford. The pretty girl's father had the right idea when he forced me to double with her male cousin. But the male cousin and his date went off by themselves as soon as we got there, and we were still alone for the night. We danced and later kissed and rubbed pelvis but still had our clothes on and no sex. (Getting a girl pregnant in those days meant you had to marry her.) We met back up after I dropped the pretty girl off at the door at 3:00 a.m. and met Janice at the parking lot. I dropped off the 1960 Ford and walked back to my car. Then Janice and I got into my car, and we both went home together with our parents none the wiser for several years.

I had stayed back and this time would not trust anyone to do my English homework and actually did it myself. Now once again, I was a graduating senior and had another prom to attend. I was asked by a shy but pretty girl to take her to the prom, and I said yes. I *should* have dated her first instead of waiting until prom night. Saul would not go and had missed his own prom because we could not double-date. Gretchen was to be my date, and she was cute but not beautiful in her gown. I was in my tuxedo, and I used my own car to pick her up. We went to the prom and took pictures and had a seat. They were serving coffee and soda, but she wanted *tea*. I asked politely, but they said they had none. She then had a minor temper tantrum, stomping her feet and pouting like a little child. She then refused to dance like I had done something wrong. All night we sat there, and in those days everyone was paired up. There was no one else to have a dance with. We stayed until the end, and I was livid, wanting nothing more than to be rid of Gretchen. When we got to her house a second time (first time, pictures), I told her mother what happened. She stated that Gretchen was a little strange sometimes but had her heart set on going to a certain after-party. I refused, but her mother was so convincing, and Gretchen apologized and said this would be different if I agreed to take her. Although, I was still a virgin, I was angry enough to force Gretchen to perform some sex act to soothe my anger. My guardian angel (Gwen) said *no*. Just wait and see, and I would be happy. I drove to the party that was at a White person's house. We were talking on the first floor, and the bar was open in the basement. She went to the basement and left me alone, and once again and I was unhappy at having agreed. After about an hour, I was told to come to the basement and get Gretchen. She had been drinking dark drinks, light drinks, wine, and anything she got her hands on. She was drunk and out of her mind. Now I was *really* angry with both with Gretchen and her mother. Somebody owed me a good time. I was again tempted to have Gretchen perform some sex act to soothe my anger and pride. Once again my guardian angel said *no*. I had to pull the car over twice so she would not puke in my car. I finally got her to her door where her mother, upon hearing the story, did not seem surprised. I left and realized that my guardian angel, Gwen, was right! Had I forced her into a sex act before going to the party, then I would always believe that I was responsible for her drinking. However, by remaining a gentleman (even an angry gentleman), it would not be on my conscience for the rest of my life. What she had done was all her.

I graduated finally but would not walk across the stage. I picked up my diploma later. I was told I cheated my mother out of seeing me walk and get my diploma. I was now ready for the world, and I said, "Here I am, world!" And the world said, "So WHAT?"

End

ABOUT THE AUTHOR

William E. Oliver Jr. was born in New England and grew up there. He went into the Armed Forces just as the Vietnam conflict/war was heating up. I survived the war and went to college, dated, married, and had two wonderful children (Lydia and Lynnette). He bought a house using the GI Bill and spent his life chasing the American dream.

CPSIA information can be obtained
at www.ICGtesting.com
Printed in the USA
LVHW090429040821
694386LV00005B/255